# The Adventures Of
# Tom Sawyer

### Mark Twain

CAMPFIRE™

**KALYANI NAVYUG MEDIA PVT LTD**

New Delhi

Sitting around the Campfire, telling the story, were:

| | | |
|---|---|---|
| **Wordsmith** | : | Matt Josdal |
| **Illustrator** | : | Brian Shearer |
| **Colorist** | : | Surya Muduli |
| **Color Consultant** | : | R. C. Prakash |
| **Letterer** | : | Bhavnath Chaudhary |
| **Editors** | : | Eman Chowdhary |
| | | Divya Dubey |
| **Research Editor** | : | Pushpanjali Borooah |

**Cover Artists:**

| | | |
|---|---|---|
| **Illustrator** | : | Naresh Kumar |
| **Colorist** | : | R. C. Prakash |
| **Designer** | : | Manishi Gupta |

Published by Kalyani Navyug Media Pvt Ltd
101 C, Shiv House, Hari Nagar Ashram
New Delhi 110014
India
www.campfire.co.in

ISBN: 978-93-80028-34-7

Printed in India at Tara Art Printers Pvt Ltd.

## About the Author

Samuel Langhorne Clemens, known to most as Mark Twain, has been hailed by many as the father of American Literature. His two most famous works, *The Adventures of Tom Sawyer* (1876) and *The Adventures of Huckleberry Finn* (1884), are considered two of the greatest American novels of all time.

Twain was born in Florida, Missouri on November 30, 1835. He grew up in the town of Hannibal on the Mississippi River, which would eventually serve as the basis for the place where Tom Sawyer and Huckleberry Finn would live.

Twain tried turning his hand to many different professions throughout his life, but continued writing all the while. His first job was as a printer's apprentice and, during this time, he met a famous steamboat captain who convinced him to become a pilot. After two years of training, he acquired his license and began traversing the mighty Mississippi as the pilot of a steamboat. It was a dangerous and lucrative form of employment.

Twain grew up in Missouri at a time when it was a slave state. After the American Civil War broke out, he became a strong supporter of emancipation, and staunchly believed that the slave trade should be abolished.

Though he began as a comic writer, the tribulations he faced in his personal life perhaps served to turn him into a serious, even pessimistic, writer in his later years. He lost his wife and two daughters, and his ill-fated life never really allowed him to recover. Twain passed away in 1910, but he is still one of the best-loved writers around the world.

Injun Joe

Huckleberry Finn

Aunt Polly

Tom Sawyer

Becky Thatcher

The old lady whirled around, snatched her skirt out of danger, and the lad fled instantly.

Saturday morning came, and all the world was bright and fresh, and brimming with life. There was a song in every heart, and music on every pair of lips.

*SIGH!*

Tom appeared with a bucket of whitewash and a long-handled brush. As he looked at the fence, the joy went out of nature and a deep sadness settled upon his spirits.

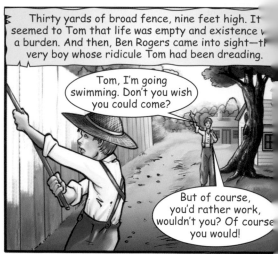

Thirty yards of broad fence, nine feet high. It seemed to Tom that life was empty and existence [w]as a burden. And then, Ben Rogers came into sight—th[e] very boy whose ridicule Tom had been dreading.

Tom, I'm going swimming. Don't you wish you could come?

But of course, you'd rather work, wouldn't you? Of course you would!

What do you call work?

Why, isn't that work?

Well, maybe it is and maybe it isn't. All I know is that it suits Tom Sawyer.

Tom's brush continued to move.

Oh, come now, you don't mean to say that you like it?

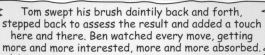

Tom swept his brush daintily back and forth, stepped back to assess the result and added a touch here and there. Ben watched every move, getting more and more interested, more and more absorbed.

Hmmmmm...

Like it? Well, I don't see why I shouldn't like it. Does a boy get a chance to whitewash a fence every day?

That put the thing in a new light, and Ben stopped nibbling his apple.

Say, Tom, let me whitewash a little.

Well, I don't know. You see, Aunt Polly is very particular about this fence, and only one in a thousand boys could do it just the way it's got to be done.

Oh, come now. Let me just try; only just a little. I'd let you, if you were me, Tom.

Ben, I'd like to, but Aunt Polly--

No, Ben. I'm afraid--

I've got it, Tom. I'll be just as careful as you. And, if you let me try, I'll give you the core of my apple.

I'll give you all of it!

Tom gave up the brush with reluctance on his face, but eagerness in his heart. And, while Ben worked and sweated in the sun, Tom munched the apple and planned how to trick more innocents.

There was no lack of material. Boys came along every now and then. They came to jeer, but stayed to whitewash.

Tom traded the next go to Billy Fisher for a kite. And when he finished, Johnny Miller bought in for a dead rat and a string to swing it with. And when the middle of the afternoon came, Tom was literally rolling in wealth.

Tom had discovered a great law of human nature, without knowing it—in order to make a person want something, you only need to make it difficult to attain.

It's not such an empty world, after all.

He had a nice, lazy time. If he hadn't run out of whitewash, he would have bankrupted every boy in the village.

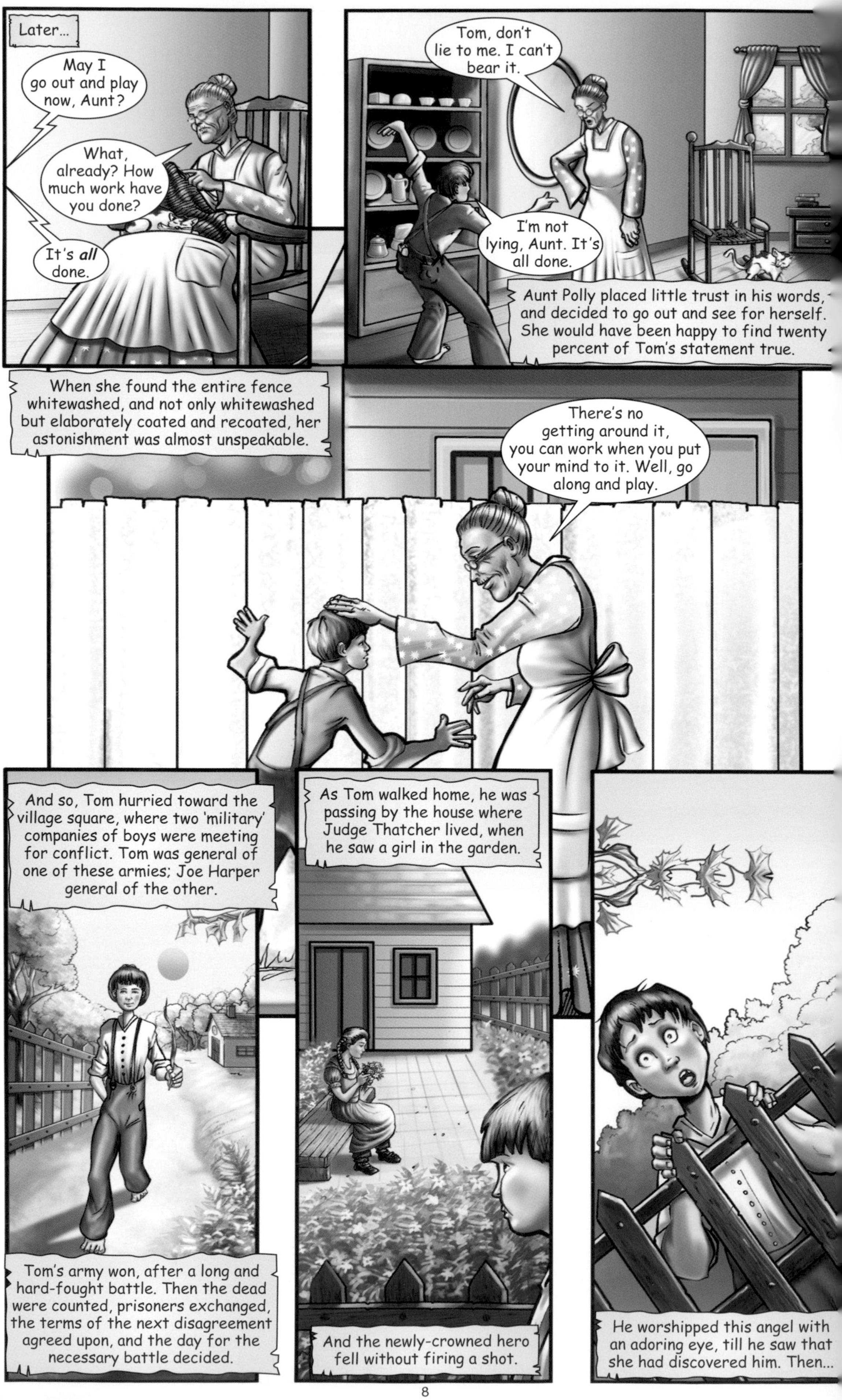
Later...
May I go out and play now, Aunt?
What, already? How much work have you done?
It's *all* done.
Tom, don't lie to me. I can't bear it.
I'm not lying, Aunt. It's all done.
Aunt Polly placed little trust in his words, and decided to go out and see for herself. She would have been happy to find twenty percent of Tom's statement true.
When she found the entire fence whitewashed, and not only whitewashed but elaborately coated and recoated, her astonishment was almost unspeakable.
There's no getting around it, you can work when you put your mind to it. Well, go along and play.
And so, Tom hurried toward the village square, where two 'military' companies of boys were meeting for conflict. Tom was general of one of these armies; Joe Harper general of the other.
Tom's army won, after a long and hard-fought battle. Then the dead were counted, prisoners exchanged, the terms of the next disagreement agreed upon, and the day for the necessary battle decided.
As Tom walked home, he was passing by the house where Judge Thatcher lived, when he saw a girl in the garden.
And the newly-crowned hero fell without firing a shot.
He worshipped this angel with an adoring eye, till he saw that she had discovered him. Then...

...he began to show off in all sorts of absurd boyish ways, in order to win her admiration.

He kept this foolishness up for some time. But, by and by, when he was in the middle of some particularly dangerous performances...

...he glanced to one side, and saw that the little girl was heading toward the house.

AAAHH

She stopped on the steps for a moment, and then moved toward the door. Tom heaved a great sigh as she stepped into the entrance. But then his face lit up...

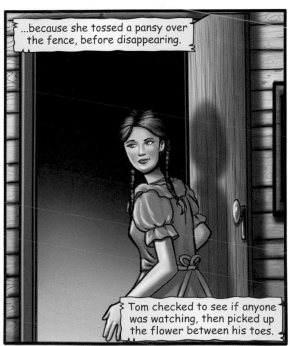

...because she tossed a pansy over the fence, before disappearing.

Tom checked to see if anyone was watching, then picked up the flower between his toes.

He hopped away with the treasure and disappeared around the corner. Then he buttoned the flower inside his shirt, next to his heart.

He returned and hung about the fence till nightfall, showing off as before.

The girl didn't show herself again, but Tom comforted himself with the hope that she had been watching through a window, and had been aware of his attentions.

On Monday morning, Tom Sawyer felt miserable because it meant the start of another week of suffering at school.

He generally began every Monday wishing he had no days off—they made going back to school so much worse.

If I were to get sick, I could stay home from school.

He checked himself, but found no ailment, so he investigated again.

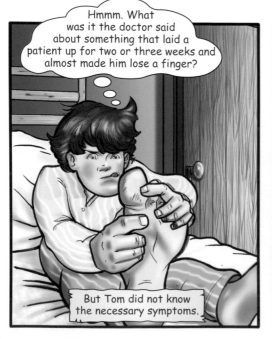

Hmmm. What was it the doctor said about something that laid a patient up for two or three weeks and almost made him lose a finger?

But Tom did not know the necessary symptoms.

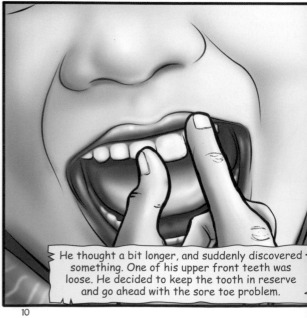

He thought a bit longer, and suddenly discovered something. One of his upper front teeth was loose. He decided to keep the tooth in reserve and go ahead with the sore toe problem.

It seemed well worth the risk, so he started groaning with considerable spirit.

OWWWWW

Tom? Tom, what's the matter with you?

Oh Aunty, my sore toe. It's become stiff!

Tom, what a turn you gave me! Now stop this nonsense and get out of bed.

The groans stopped, and the pain vanished from the toe. Feeling a little foolish, Tom quickly switched to the reserve plan.

But, Aunt Polly, my tooth!

Your tooth, indeed! What's the matter with your tooth?

It's loose, and it aches awfully.

Aunt Polly quickly got the dental instruments ready.

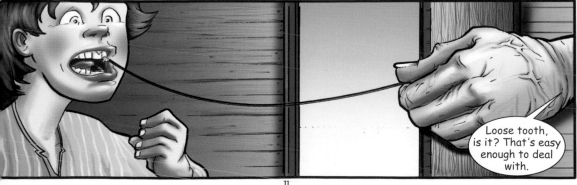

Loose tooth, is it? That's easy enough to deal with.

There. Off to school with you now.

OOWWWWWW!!

On his way to school, Tom came across the young outcast of the village; the son of the town drunkard.

Hello, Huckleberry Finn!

Hello yourself.

What's that you got?

A dead cat.

Let me see him, Huck.

My, he's pretty stiff. Where did you get him?

Bought him off a boy.

Say, what are dead cats good for, Huck?

Good for? For curing warts, of course!

How do you cure warts with dead cats?

You take your cat and go to the graveyard at about midnight, where somebody wicked has been buried.

And when it's midnight, a devil will come, or maybe two or three, but you can't see them. You can only hear something like the wind, or maybe hear them talk.

And when they are taking the body away, you heave your cat after them and say, 'devil follow corpse, cat follow devil, wart follow cat, I'm done with you.' That will cure any wart.

Sounds good. Say, Hucky, when are you going to take the cat to the graveyard?

Tonight.

Can I go with you?

Of course, if you aren't afraid.

Afraid? That isn't likely, Will you meow?

Yes, and you meow back if you get a chance. Last time you kept me meowing till people started throwing rocks at me, thinking I was a cat!

I'll meow this time, Huck.

When he finally reached the school, he strode in briskly, as if he'd been trying his best not to be late.

Thomas Sawyer!

Tom knew that when his name was pronounced in full, it meant trouble.

Yes, sir?

Come up here at once, and you can explain why you're late, as usual!

And where were you?

Tom was about to take refuge in a lie, when he saw two long tails of yellow hair, which he recognized due to the feeling of love.

Uhhh... that is I... ummm

13

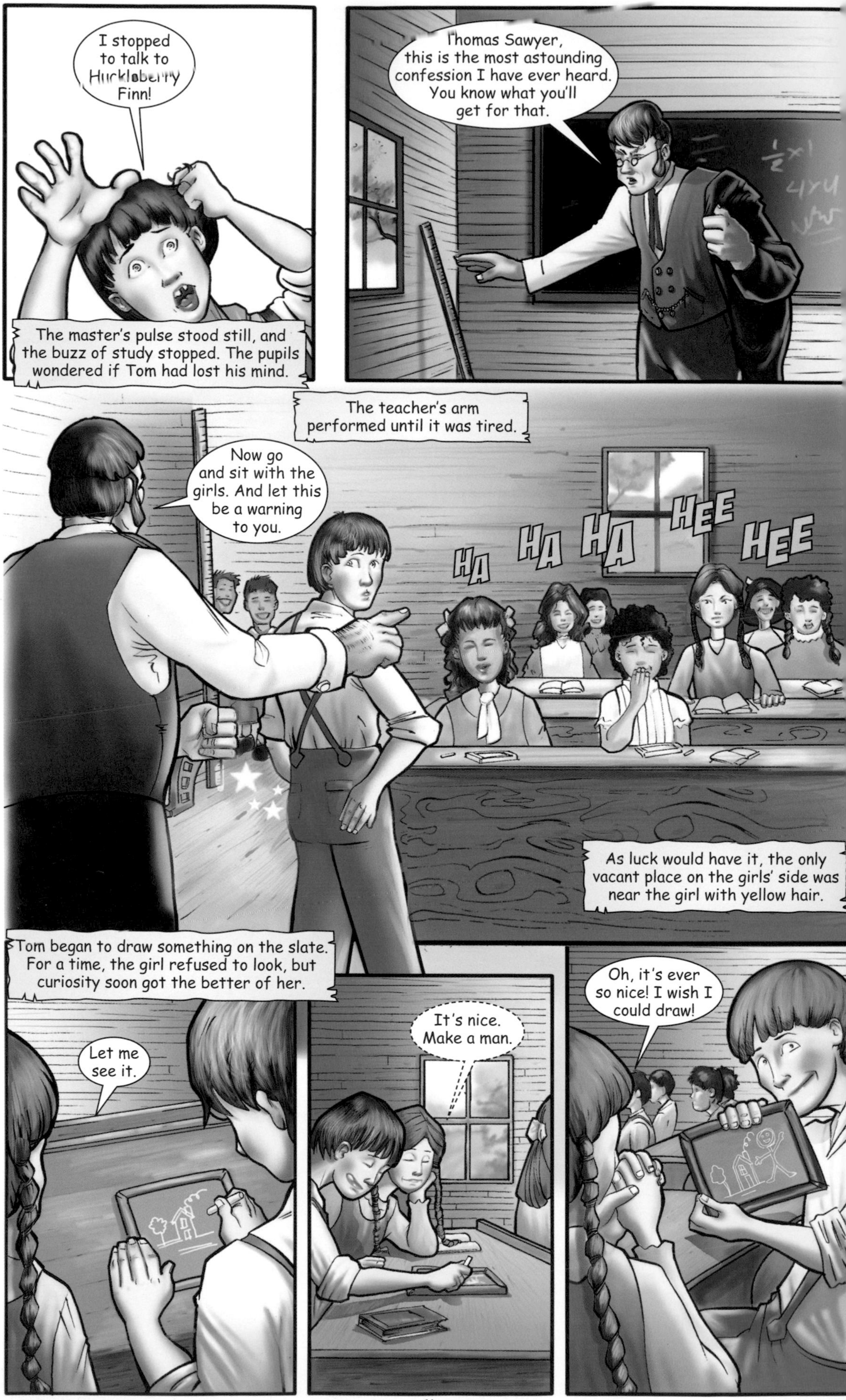
I stopped to talk to Huckleberry Finn!
The master's pulse stood still, and the buzz of study stopped. The pupils wondered if Tom had lost his mind.
Thomas Sawyer, this is the most astounding confession I have ever heard. You know what you'll get for that.
The teacher's arm performed until it was tired.
Now go and sit with the girls. And let this be a warning to you.
HA HA HA HEE HEE
As luck would have it, the only vacant place on the girls' side was near the girl with yellow hair.
Tom began to draw something on the slate. For a time, the girl refused to look, but curiosity soon got the better of her.
Let me see it.
It's nice. Make a man.
Oh, it's ever so nice! I wish I could draw!

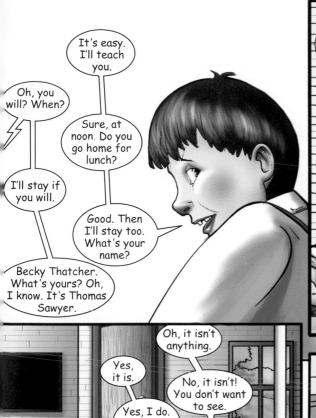

It's easy. I'll teach you.

Oh, you will? When?

Sure, at noon. Do you go home for lunch?

I'll stay if you will.

Good. Then I'll stay too. What's your name?

Becky Thatcher. What's yours? Oh, I know. It's Thomas Sawyer.

That's the name they punish me with. I'm Tom when I'm good. You call me Tom, will you?

Yes. What's that there?

Oh, it isn't anything.

Yes, it is.

No, it isn't! You don't want to see.

Yes, I do. Please let me see.

No, I won't—I promise I won't.

You'll tell.

Becky hit his hand, but blushed and looked pleased nevertheless.

Oh, you bad thing!

Oh! You don't want to see--

I LOVE YOU

At that moment, Tom was dragged across the room, under a peppering fire of giggles.

Although his ear tingled, his heart was jubilant.

Tom held Becky's hand in his, guiding it, until she had created a house. When the interest in art started to wane, the two began talking. Tom was swimming in bliss.

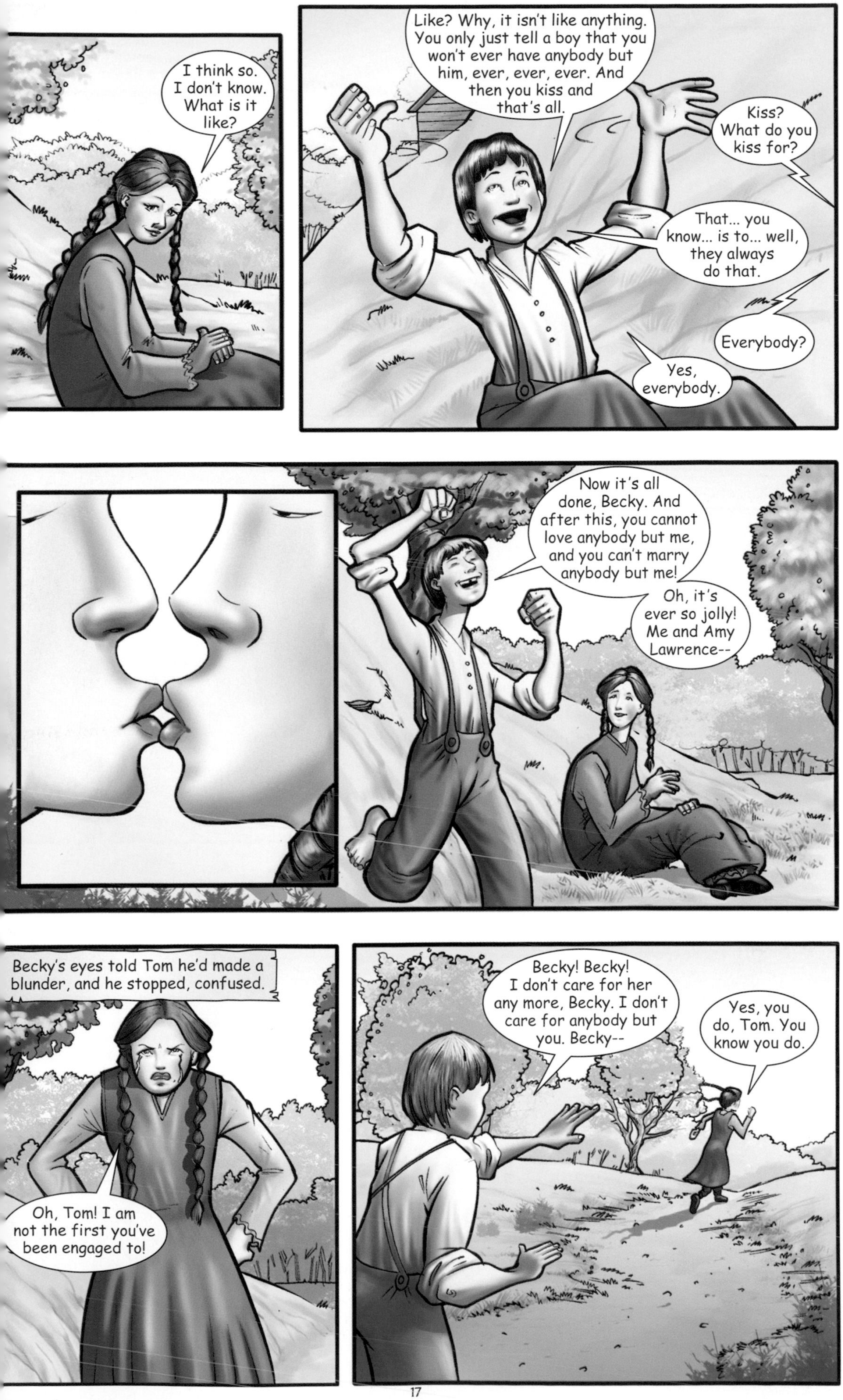
I think so. I don't know. What is it like?
Like? Why, it isn't like anything. You only just tell a boy that you won't ever have anybody but him, ever, ever, ever. And then you kiss and that's all.
Kiss? What do you kiss for?
That... you know... is to... well, they always do that.
Everybody?
Yes, everybody.
Now it's all done, Becky. And after this, you cannot love anybody but me, and you can't marry anybody but me!
Oh, it's ever so jolly! Me and Amy Lawrence--
Becky's eyes told Tom he'd made a blunder, and he stopped, confused.
Oh, Tom! I am not the first you've been engaged to!
Becky! Becky! I don't care for her any more, Becky. I don't care for anybody but you. Becky--
Yes, you do, Tom. You know you do.

Drat!

With Tom's mood ruined by the failed engagement, he decided that school was the last place he wanted to be.

Then Tom marched over the hills and far away.

But the elastic heart of youth cannot be kept compressed into one shape for long. Tom's mind soon began to drift off.

Doodle-bug, doodle-bug, tell me what I want to know! Doodle-bug, doodle-bug, tell me what I want to know!

Tom was lost in his thoughts, when Joe Harper appeared.

Hold! Who comes here into Sherwood Forest without my permission?

It is I, Sir Guy of Guisborne. Who are you that... that...

...dares to hold such language.

Who are you that dares to hold such language?

It is I, Robin Hood, as your dead body shall soon know!

Are you indeed that famous outlaw? I will gladly dispute the passes of the wood with you.

Tom, you can be Friar Tuck; or I'll be the Sheriff of Nottingham, and you be Robin Hood and kill me.

This was a satisfactory suggestion, and so these adventures were carried out.

Joe, I'd rather be an outlaw in Sherwood for one year, than President of the United States forever.

Me too, Tom. Me too.

On that note, the boys headed home.

At half-past nine that night, Tom went to bed as usual. He said his prayers, and lay awake, waiting in restless impatience.

TICK TOCK
TICK TOCK

The ticking of the clock became noticeable. Old beams began to crack mysteriously and the stairs creaked faintly. Evidently spirits were outside.

Next, the ghastly ticking of a death-watch beetle in the wall made Tom shudder—it meant that somebody's days were numbered.

MEEOOOWW

And then there came, mingling with his half-formed dreams, a most distressing noise.

Scat! You devil!

CRASH!

A minute later, Tom was dressed and out of the window.

Hi there, Hucky.

Let's get going then.

Hucky, do you think the dead people like us being here?

I wish I knew. It's awfully solemn, isn't it?

It is. Say, Hucky, do you think Hoss Williams hears us talking?

Of course he does. At least his spirit does.

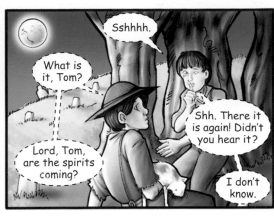

Sshhhh.

What is it, Tom?

Lord, Tom, are the spirits coming?

Shh. There it is again! Didn't you hear it?

I don't know.

Tom, they aren't spirits. They're humans. It's old Muff Potter, Injun Joe, and young Doc Robinson.

That's the talk.

Now the stubborn thing's ready, Doctor. And you need to pay us another five, or she'll stay here.

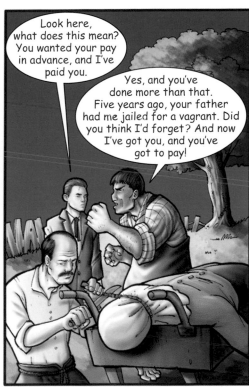

Look here, what does this mean? You wanted your pay in advance, and I've paid you.

Yes, and you've done more than that. Five years ago, your father had me jailed for a vagrant. Did you think I'd forget? And now I've got you, and you've got to pay!

All at once...

SNAP!

...the doctor seized the heavy headboard of a grave...

THUD

...and knocked Potter to the earth with it.

ARRGGGHHHH

In the same instant, Injun Joe saw his chance, and drove a knife into the doctor's chest.

21

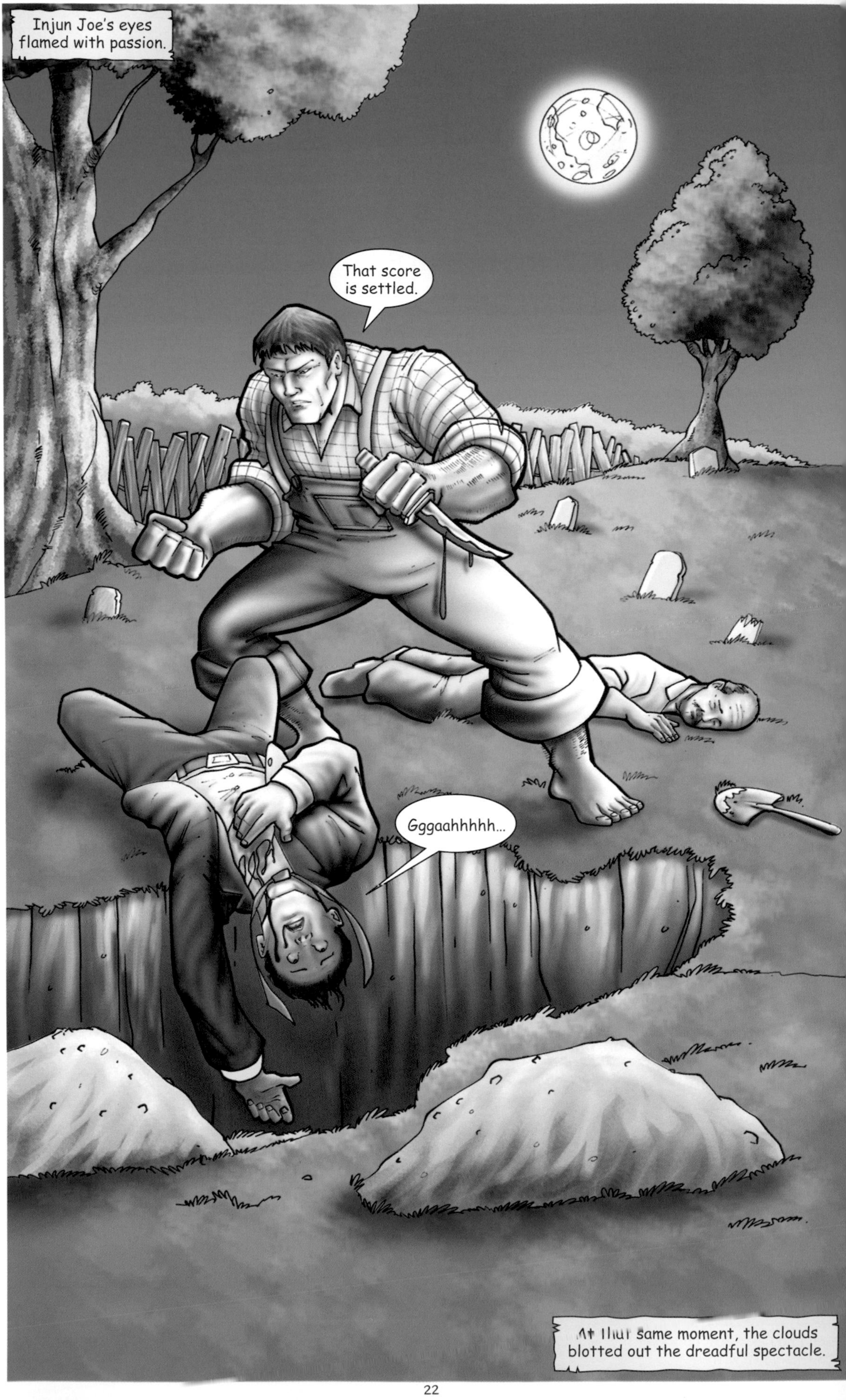

Injun Joe's eyes flamed with passion.
That score is settled.
Gggaahhhhh...
At that same moment, the clouds blotted out the dreadful spectacle.

Come on, Tom. Move it!

I'm right behind you, Hucky!

Injun Joe robbed the body, and put the murder weapon in Potter's right hand.

After five minutes, Potter began to stir and moan. Then his hand closed upon the knife.

What is this, Joe?

It's a dirty business. What did you do it for?

I-I did not do it!

Look here, that kind of talk won't work.

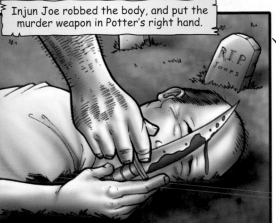

I shouldn't have had a drink tonight. I'm all in a muddle; I can't remember anything about it. Tell me Joe—honest now—did I do it?

You snatched up that knife and jammed it into him, just as he was about to hit you again. And here you've laid, dead as a doornail till now.

I didn't know what I was doing. It was all because of the whiskey and the excitement, I think.

I always liked you, Joe, and stood up for you. Don't you remember? You won't tell, will you, Joe?

Come now, that's enough of that. This isn't any time for crying. You go that way and I'll go this. And don't leave any tracks behind you.

No. You've always been fair and square with me, Muff Potter, and I'll be fair to you.

The two boys ran to the village, speechless with horror.

Huck, what do you think will come of this?

If Doctor Robinson dies, I think there'll be a hanging.

Who'll tell? Should we?

What are you talking about? Suppose something happened and Injun Joe didn't hang, he'd kill us sooner or later.

That's just what I was thinking to myself, Huck.

If anybody tells, let Muff Potter do it, if he's foolish enough. He's generally drunk enough.

Huck, Muff Potter doesn't know anything.

But, why doesn't he know?

Because he had just got that whack when Injun Joe did it. Do you think he could see anything? Do you think he knows anything?

By hokey, you're right, Tom!

Hucky, you sure we can keep mum about this?

Tom, we got to keep mum. You know that. Injun Joe would drown us like a couple of cats if we squeal about this and he doesn't get hanged.

Now Tom, let us swear to one another—that's what we got to do—swear to keep mum.

I agree, Huck. Let's just hold hands and swear that we--

Oh no, that won't do for this. That's good enough for little rubbishy common things—especially with girls—but we should be writing about a big thing like this. In blood!

Right.

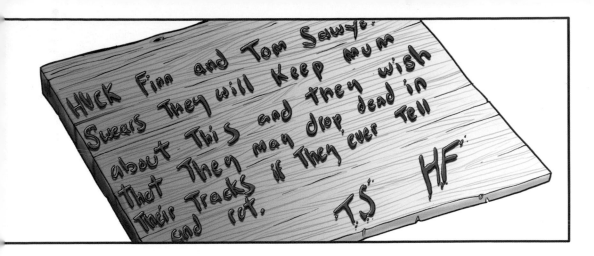

When Tom crept into his bedroom, the night was almost over. He fell asleep, congratulating himself that nobody knew of his escapade.

Everyone drifted toward the graveyard and Tom joined the procession. He would rather have gone anywhere else, but an awful, inexplicable fascination drew him on.

It's him, it's Potter. He's coming himself!

Don't let him get away!

Upon my word and honor friends, I didn't do it.

Hellish fiend. He wanted to come and take a quiet look at his work, but didn't expect any company, I bet.

Oh, Injun Joe, you promised me you'd never...

Tell them, Joe, tell them!

Why didn't you leave? What did you come here for?

I couldn't help it. I wanted to run away, but I couldn't seem to come anywhere but here.

I saw it all. Potter grabbed his knife and stabbed the Doc right in the chest. That's it.

Joe! Joe! I didn't do it! Joe!

26

Tom's fearful secret, and gnawing conscience, disturbed him for a week after that.

It seemed to Tom that his schoolmates would never stop holding inquests on dead cats. But he couldn't take his mind off his troubles.

He had no interest in joining his friends, and that was strange.

Every day, during this time of sorrow, Tom went to the little jail window and smuggled as many small luxuries through to the 'murderer' as he could get hold of.

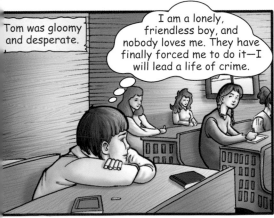

Tom was gloomy and desperate.

I am a lonely, friendless boy, and nobody loves me. They have finally forced me to do it—I will lead a life of crime.

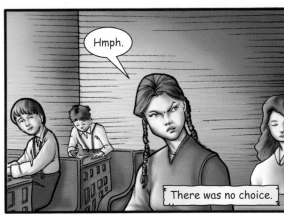

Hmph.

There was no choice.

After school, Tom met his closest comrade, Joe Harper. They were two souls with a single thought.

Why are you so glum, Tom?

That's it, Joe, I'm giving it all up. I'm leaving forever; I'm off to be a pirate.

Why, Tom, I was just about to come looking for you! I have been whipped for drinking cream I didn't touch. I'm off to be a hermit and was looking for some company.

But, Joe, just think of the adventures a pirate has! A hermit just goes off and dies all alone.

After listening to Tom, Joe accepted that there were some real advantages to a life of crime, and so he agreed to be a pirate.

Right then. But if we're to be a true band of pirates, we'll need one more. We should ask...

Huckleberry Finn!

Sure. Sounds good. We'll all gather what we can and head for Jackson's Island at midnight.

At about midnight, Tom arrived with a boiled ham and a few trifles. It was starlight, and very still. The mighty river lay like an ocean at rest. Tom listened for a moment, but no sound disturbed the quiet.

MEEOOOW

Who goes there?

Tom Sawyer, the Black Avenger of the Spanish Main. Name your names.

Huck Finn, the Red-Handed!

Joe Harper, the Terror of the Seas!

That's good. Give the countersign.

BLOOD!

The Terror of the Seas had brought a side of bacon, and had worn himself out getting it there. Finn, the Red-Handed, had stolen a frying pan and a quantity of leaf tobacco. He had also brought a few corn cobs to make pipes with.

Soon they shoved off.

Yes, sir.

Bring her to the wind!

What sail's she carrying?

Courses, top sails, and flying-jib, sir!

The Black Avenger stood looking, for the last time, upon the scene of his former joys and later sufferings. He wished 'she' could see him now, out on the wild sea.

You see, a pirate doesn't have to do anything when he's ashore, Joe.

But a hermit has to pray all the time, and he doesn't have any fun, anyway. And he is all by himself.

Oh, yes, that's true. But I haven't thought much about it, you know. I'd much rather be a pirate, now that I've tried it.

It was a glorious feeling to be wild and free in the forest of an unexplored and uninhabited island, far from mankind. The boys decided never to return to civilization.

What do pirates have to do?

Oh, they have a terrific time. They take ships and burn them, and get the money and bury it in awful places, and make everyone from the ships walk the plank.

And they wear the greatest clothes! All gold and silver and diamonds.

I'm not dressed fit for a pirate, but these are the only clothes I have.

Shucks, Hucky... you'll... be just... zzzz... fine... zzzzzz...

Tom, I reckon I just will...

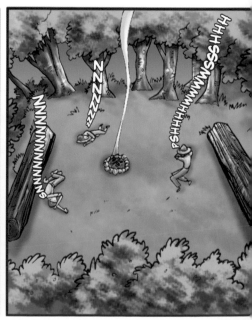

When Tom awoke in the morning, he wondered where he was. He looked around, thought for a while and then remembered.

The marvel of nature waking up and going to work showed itself to Tom.

Yo-ho me lads!

He stirred up the other pirates and they all clattered away with a shout.

In a minute or two, they were stripped and chasing after each other in the shallow, clear water. They felt no longing for the little village sleeping in the distance, beyond the majestic stretch of water.

They found a promising nook in the river bank and threw in their lines. Almost immediately, they got a reward.

They came back to camp wonderfully refreshed, glad-hearted, and ravenous.

Soon, however, talk ran slow. The stillness and solemnity in the woods, and the sense of loneliness, began to tell upon the spirits of the boys.

For some time, the boys had been aware of a peculiar sound in the distance, but then...

BOOM

What is it?

It isn't thunder!

What else can it be?

Let's go and see.

BOOM

Now I know what's happened! Somebody's drowned!

That's it. They did that last summer when Bill Turner drowned.

They shoot a cannon over the water, and that makes him come up to the top. And they take loaves of bread and put mercury in them and set them afloat. Wherever there's anybody that's drowned, they'll float right there and stop.

By jings, I wish I was over there now.

I do, too. I'd give heaps to know who it is.

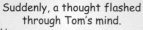

Suddenly, a thought flashed through Tom's mind.

Boys, I know who's drowned— it's us!

Hurray!

Whoop!

Yee-haw!!

They felt like heroes. They were missed; they were mourned; hearts were breaking on their account; tears were being shed; and best of all, they were the talk of the whole town, and the envy of all the other boys.

It was worth being a pirate after all.

As twilight drew on, the ferry boat went back to her usual business and the skifs disappeared. The pirates were jubilant over their new grandeur and the trouble they were causing.

By and by, Joe decided to find out what the others might think about a return to civilization.

Say, boys, what are your thoughts about going back? Maybe not tonight, but...

Boooo.

Noooooo, Joe.

Alright, alright.

Mutiny was laid to rest for the moment.

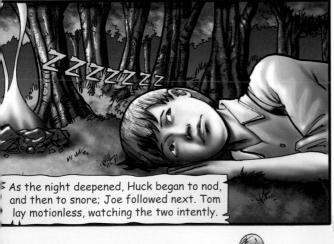

ZZZZZZZz

As the night deepened, Huck began to nod, and then to snore; Joe followed next. Tom lay motionless, watching the two intently.

Some time later, he made his way cautiously, till he was out of hearing distance. Then, he broke into a run in the direction of the river. Before leaving, he wrote a message for his mates in the sand.

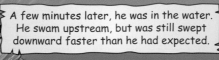

A few minutes later, he was in the water. He swam upstream, but was still swept downward faster than he had expected.

However, he finally reached the shore, and went straight to his house.

What makes the candle blow? That door's open, I believe. Of course, it is. No end of strange things happening.

Tom wasn't bad—just mischievous. Just giddy, and reckless. He was less responsible than a colt. He never meant any harm, and he was the best-hearted boy that ever was.

If the bodies are still missing by Sunday, all hope will be gone, and the funerals will take place that morning.

Then Aunt Polly prayed for Tom so touchingly, so appealingly, and with such measureless love in her words and her old trembling voice...

...that Tom was in tears.

Straightaway he made his stealthy exit, latching the door behind him.

The night was over and it was broad daylight before he found himself close to the island.

Tom's true blue, Huck, and he'll come back. He won't desert us. He knows that would be a disgrace to a pirate, and Tom's too proud for that sort of thing. He's up to something or the other. I wonder what.

The rules say his things are ours if he isn't back here before breakfast.

Which he is!

A sumptuous breakfast of bacon and fish was soon provided. After the boys had finished it off, Tom recounted (and exaggerated) his adventures.

But, as time passed, interest waned.

Oh boys, let's give it up. I want to go home. It's so lonesome.

Oh no, Joe, you'll feel better soon. Just think of the fishing we'll do.

I don't care for the fishing. I want to go home.

But Joe, there isn't such a good place to swim anywhere else.

Swimming's no good. I don't care for it when there isn't anybody to tell me not to do it! I'm going home.

Oh, shucks! Baby! You want to see your mother, I guess.

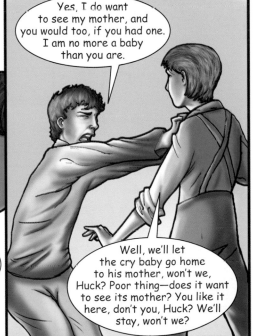

Yes, I do want to see my mother, and you would too, if you had one. I am no more a baby than you are.

Well, we'll let the cry baby go home to his mother, won't we, Huck? Poor thing—does it want to see its mother? You like it here, don't you, Huck? We'll stay, won't we?

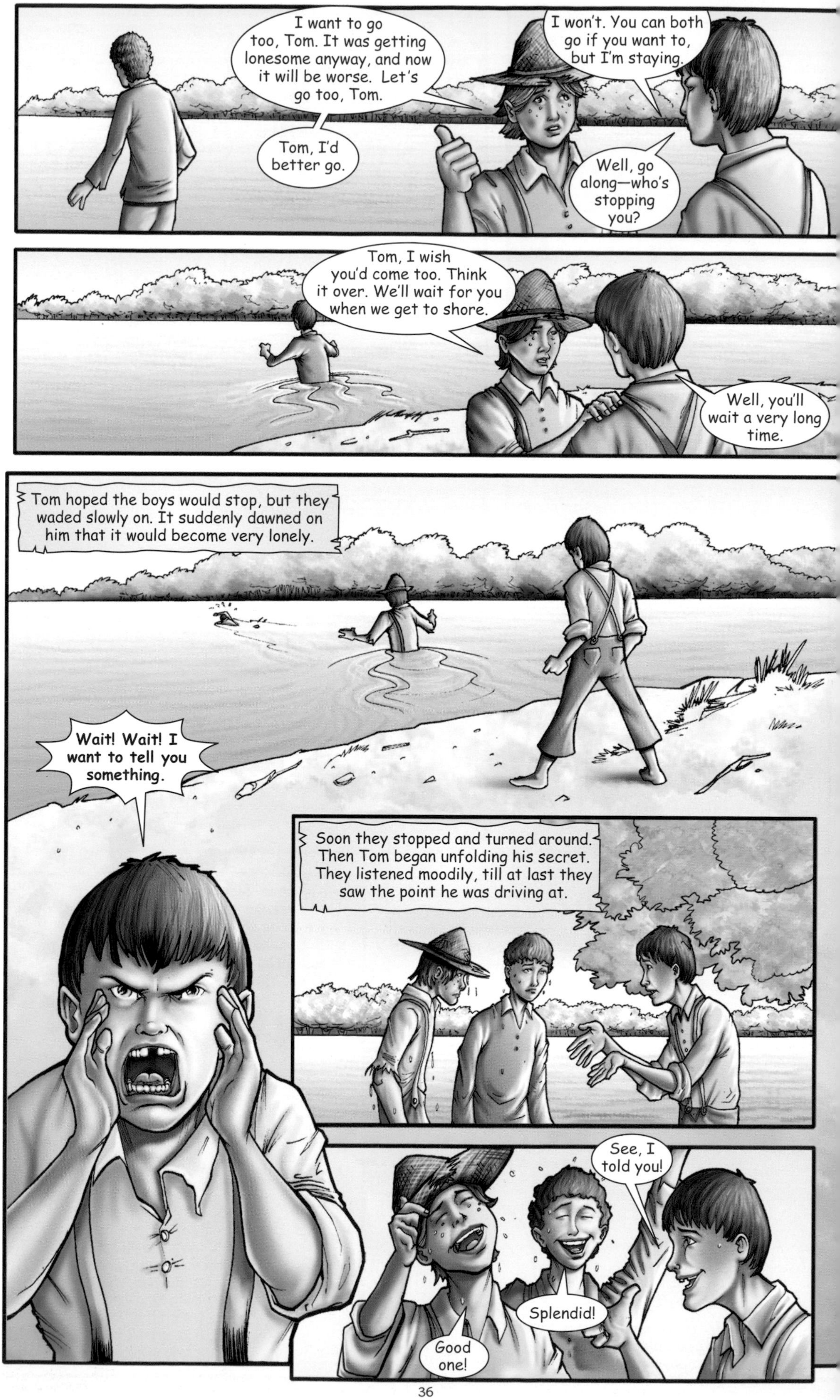
I want to go too, Tom. It was getting lonesome anyway, and now it will be worse. Let's go too, Tom.
Tom, I'd better go.
I won't. You can both go if you want to, but I'm staying.
Well, go along—who's stopping you?
Tom, I wish you'd come too. Think it over. We'll wait for you when we get to shore.
Well, you'll wait a very long time.
Tom hoped the boys would stop, but they waded slowly on. It suddenly dawned on him that it would become very lonely.
Wait! Wait! I want to tell you something.
Soon they stopped and turned around. Then Tom began unfolding his secret. They listened moodily, till at last they saw the point he was driving at.
See, I told you!
Splendid!
Good one!

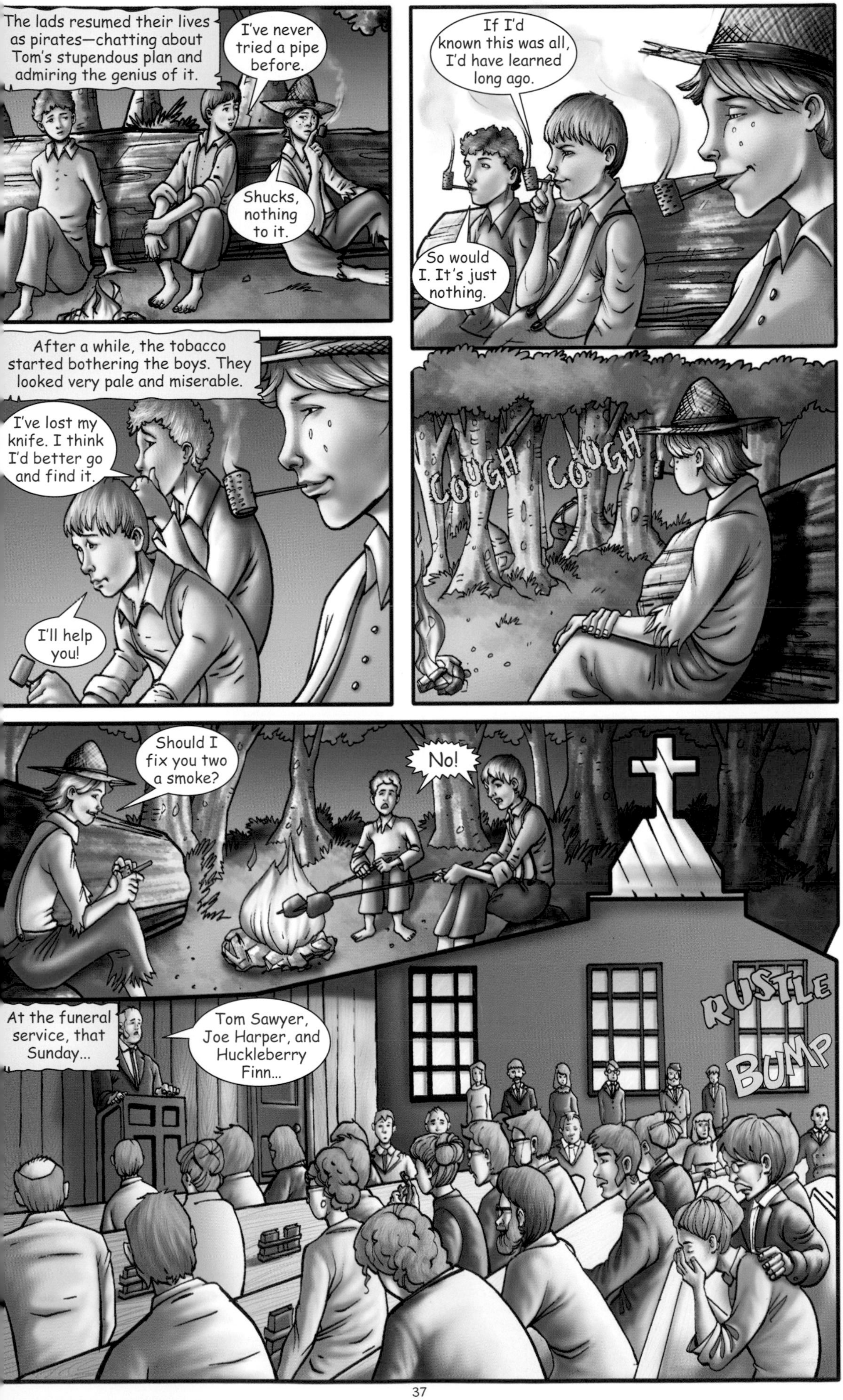

The lads resumed their lives as pirates—chatting about Tom's stupendous plan and admiring the genius of it.
I've never tried a pipe before.
Shucks, nothing to it.
If I'd known this was all, I'd have learned long ago.
So would I. It's just nothing.
After a while, the tobacco started bothering the boys. They looked very pale and miserable.
I've lost my knife. I think I'd better go and find it.
I'll help you!
COUGH COUGH
Should I fix you two a smoke?
No!
At the funeral service, that Sunday...
Tom Sawyer, Joe Harper, and Huckleberry Finn...
RUSTLE
BUMP

...I am the resurrection and I am the life...

CRETAAKK

Every pair of eyes followed the minister's. The whole congregation stared...

Good Lord!

Ahh, mercy!

...as the three dead boys came marching up the aisle. They had been hiding in the unused gallery, listening to their own funeral sermon.

Aunt Polly and the Harpers threw themselves upon their loved ones, smothered them with kisses and poured out thanksgivings.

Oh, my boy.

Joe, Joe!

Meanwhile, poor Huck stood looking uncomfortable. He didn't know what to do or where to hide from so many unwelcoming eyes.

Aunt Polly, it isn't fair. Somebody's got to be glad to see Huck!

And so they shall! I'm glad to see him, the poor motherless thing.

Tom got more cuffs and kisses that day—depending on Aunt Polly's varying moods—than he'd had all year.

Praise God from whom all blessings flow. Sing everyone, and put your hearts into it.

That was Tom's great secret—the scheme to return home with his fellow pirates and attend their own funerals!

What a hero Tom became. He did not skip and prance about. Instead, he moved with a dignified swagger, suitable to a pirate who had caught the public eye.

He pretended not to see the looks or hear the remarks as he walked along, but he enjoyed every one of them.

Then, one day, as Tom was on his way to school, he came upon Becky Thatcher.

I've acted mean, Becky, and I'm sorry. I won't ever do that again as long as I live. Please make up with me, won't you?

I'll thank you to keep to yourself, Mr. Thomas Sawyer. I'll never speak to you again.

She tossed her head and walked away.

Tom was so stunned, he didn't even have the presence of mind to say 'Who cares, Miss Smarty?' until the right time to say it had gone.

But Becky did not know how fast she was nearing trouble herself.

CREAK

ANATOMY

Every day, Mr. Dobbins, the schoolmaster, took a mysterious book out of his desk, and absorbed himself in it when the class were working in silence.

Becky found herself in the classroom. She glanced around, and the next instant she had the book in her hands.

RRRIIIPPP

At that moment, the door opened and Tom peeped in. Becky put the book back in the drawer, tearing it in the process.

Tom Sawyer, you are just as mean as you can be, to sneak up on a person and look at what they're looking at!

Be mean if you want to, Tom Sawyer.

How could I know you were looking at anything?

You should be ashamed of yourself. You are going to tell on me, and then what will I do! I'll be whipped, and I have never been whipped in school before.

A few minutes later, the master arrived and the class began. After a while, he straightened himself up, yawned...

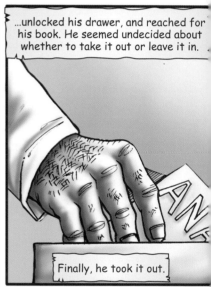

...unlocked his drawer, and reached for his book. He seemed undecided about whether to take it out or leave it in.

Finally, he took it out.

WHO TORE THIS BOOK?

There was not a sound. You could have heard a pin drop.

THUD

The stillness continued. The master searched every face for signs of guilt.

Benjamin Rogers, did you tear this book? Or was it you, Amy Lawrence?

A denial. Another pause.

40

Gracie Miller? Susan Harper, did you do this? Rebecca Thatcher? Look me in the face!

Another denial.

Tom's uneasiness grew more and more intense under the slow torture of these proceedings. Suddenly, a thought shot like lightning through his brain. He sprang to his feet and shouted...

I did it!

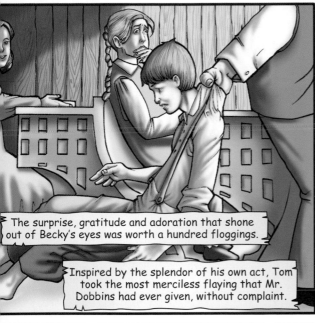

The surprise, gratitude and adoration that shone out of Becky's eyes was worth a hundred floggings.

Inspired by the splendor of his own act, Tom took the most merciless flaying that Mr. Dobbins had ever given, without complaint.

He also received the added cruelty of having to stay for two hours after school.

Tom, how could you be so noble?

Days passed without much happening.

But then, at last, the sleepy atmosphere in the village was vigorously stirred. The murder trial started in court. It immediately became the absorbing topic of conversation throughout the village.

Tom could not get away from it.

Well, the murder trial starts today.

Yes.

41

Huck, have you ever told anybody about that?

About what?

You know what!

Oh! Of course I haven't.

Never a word?

Never a solitary word, but what makes you ask?

Well, I was afraid.

Why, Tom, we wouldn't live for two days if that got found out. You know that.

Tom felt more comfortable.

What talk is going around, Huck? I've heard a lot of it.

Talk? Why, it's Muff Potter, Muff Potter, Potter, Potter all the time. It keeps me in a sweat, constantly. So I want to hide somewhere.

That's just the same way they talk around me. I think he's a goner. Don't you feel sorry for him sometimes?

Almost always. He isn't any good. But then he hasn't ever done anything to hurt anybody.

He gave me half a fish once, when there wasn't enough for two. And lots of times he has stood by me when I was out of luck.

He mended kites for me, Huck, and knitted hooks onto my line. I wish we could get him out of there.

We can't do anything to get him out, Tom. And besides, it wouldn't do any good. They'd catch him again.

The boys had a long talk, but it brought little comfort. They found themselves hanging about the little isolated jail, perhaps with the hope that something would happen that might sort out their difficulties.

But nothing happened. There seemed to be no angels or fairies interested in this unfortunate prisoner. The boys did as they had done before—went to the cell and gave Potter some tobacco and matches.

You've been mighty good to me boys—better than anybody else in this town.

Don't you ever get drunk. Then you won't ever end up in here. Shake my hand, boys. You've helped Muff Potter and you'd help him more if you could.

Tom and Huck were speechless.

Night, Hucky.

Night, Tom.

Tom went home, miserable, and that night his dreams were full of horrors.

All the village flocked to the court the next morning, for that was to be a great day. The trial of a murderer!

What did you see, sir?

I saw him washing his hands that very morning.

The witness is yours.

I have no questions to ask him.

And you, sir?

I saw the knife. It was Muff's—right by Doc's body.

The witness is yours.

I have no questions to ask him.

Several witnesses then made declarations concerning Potter's guilty behavior when brought to the scene of the murder.

By the oaths of citizens whose simple word is above suspicion, we have fastened this awful crime, beyond all possibility of question, upon the unhappy prisoner at the bar. We rest our case here.

A painful silence reigned in the courtroom. Many men were moved, and the compassion of many women was shown by their tears.

Your honor, in our remarks at the opening of this trial, we made our purpose clear—to prove that our client did this fearful deed while under the influence of drink. We have changed our mind. We shall not offer that plea.

Call Thomas Sawyer.

GASP

OH!

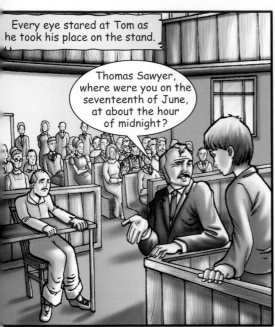

Every eye stared at Tom as he took his place on the stand.

Thomas Sawyer, where were you on the seventeenth of June, at about the hour of midnight?

In the graveyard.

A little bit louder, please. Don't be afraid. You were--

**In the graveyard!**

Now, my boy, tell us everything that occurred. Tell it in your own way, but don't skip anything, and don't be afraid.

Tom began, hesitantly at first. But, as he warmed to his subject, his words flowed more and more easily.

...and then, as the doctor picked the board up and Muff Potter fell, Injun Joe jumped with the knife and--

CRASH

As quick as lightning, Injun Joe sprang through the window, and was gone.

Hurrah!

Nice job, young Sawyer!

That was a brave thing to do, lad.

Tom was a glittering hero once more—the darling of the old, the envy of the young. His name even went into immortal print.

VILLAGE RECORD

T. SAWYER FREES MUFF POTTER!

During the days, Muff Potter's gratitude was enough to make Tom glad he had spoken.

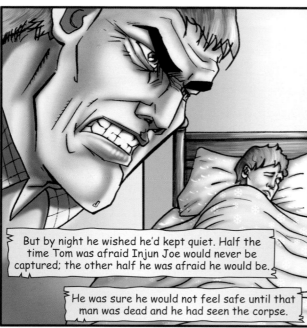

But by night he wished he'd kept quiet. Half the time Tom was afraid Injun Joe would never be captured; the other half he was afraid he would be.

He was sure he would not feel safe until that man was dead and he had seen the corpse.

Reward had been offered, and the country had been searched, but Injun Joe was not found.

One of those all-knowing and awe-inspiring marvels, a detective, came up from St. Louis. He found a clue, but you can't hang a clue for murder. So, after the detective had finished and gone home, Tom felt just as insecure as before.

The slow days drifted on, and each day the fear in Tom's heart reduced.

And, in time, boyhood seemed to return to normal.

There comes a time in every boy's life when he has a raging desire to look for buried treasure. This desire suddenly came upon Tom one day. Soon enough, he found a willing companion.

Huck Finn, the Red-Handed.

Where will we dig?

Oh, almost anywhere.

Huck was always willing to take part in any enterprise that offered entertainment and required no capital. He had lots of the sort of time which does not require money.

Why, is it hidden all around?

No, it isn't. It's hidden in particular places, Huck. Sometimes on islands, sometimes in rotten chests under the branches of dead trees, but mostly under the floor in haunted houses.

Who hides it, Tom?

Why, robbers of course—who'd you think? Sunday school teachers?

I don't know. If it was mine I wouldn't hide it. I'd spend it and have a good time.

There's the old haunted house, and there are lots of dead-branch trees—absolutely loads of them.

Is it under all of them?

Don't be silly. No!

Then how do you know which one to go for?

We'll just try all of them.

Say, Huck, if we find treasure here, what are you going to do with your share?

So they chose a new spot and began again. The labor dragged a little, but they made progress. They dug away in silence for some time.

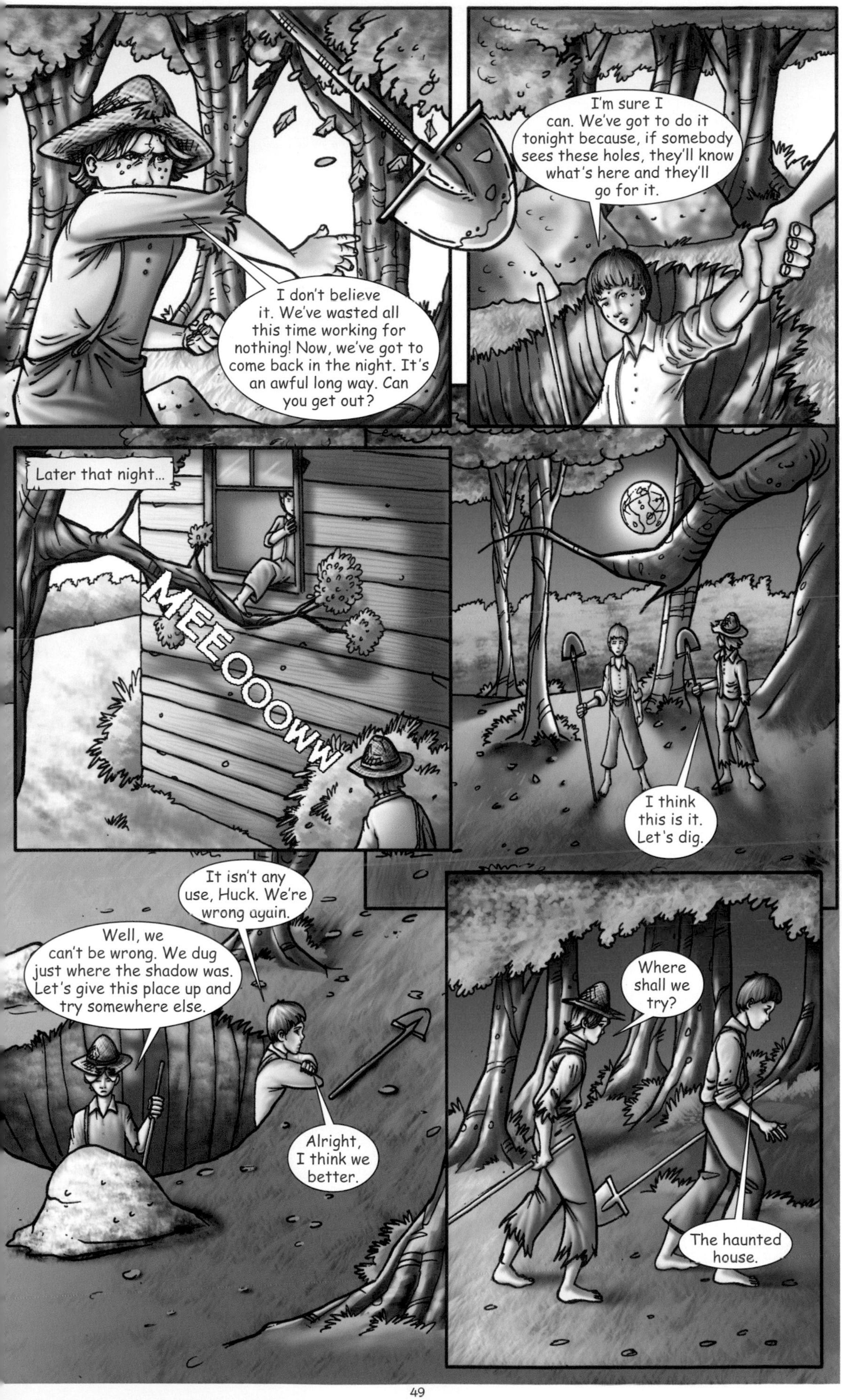
I don't believe it. We've wasted all this time working for nothing! Now, we've got to come back in the night. It's an awful long way. Can you get out?
I'm sure I can. We've got to do it tonight because, if somebody sees these holes, they'll know what's here and they'll go for it.
Later that night...
MEEOOOWW
I think this is it. Let's dig.
It isn't any use, Huck. We're wrong again.
Well, we can't be wrong. We dug just where the shadow was. Let's give this place up and try somewhere else.
Alright, I think we better.
Where shall we try?
The haunted house.

Darn it. I don't like haunted houses, Tom. They are a sight worse than dead people.

Dead people might talk, but they don't come sliding around in a shroud when you aren't looking and peep over your shoulder all of a sudden.

We'll try it during the day. Ghosts don't come around then.

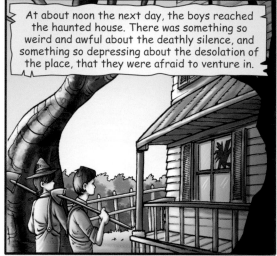

At about noon the next day, the boys reached the haunted house. There was something so weird and awful about the deathly silence, and something so depressing about the desolation of the place, that they were afraid to venture in.

They entered softly, with quickened pulses, talking in whispers, ears alert to catch the slightest sound, and muscles tense and ready for instant retreat.

What was that?

I don't know.

CREAK

Sshhh.

Scared?

No.

Then I dare you to go up.

Look. There's the old Spaniard that's been about town once or twice lately. I never saw the other man before.

I've thought it over, and I don't like it. It's dangerous.

Dangerous? Coward!

The voice made the boys gasp and quake.

50

Injun Joe!

I'll have a look around town to make sure everything is good, and then we can do this 'dangerous' job. Then we'll leg it to Texas.

What'll we do with the stolen goods we've got left?

I don't know. Leave them here as we've always done, I think. No use taking them away till we move south.

Injun Joe started digging...

CHUNK

...and then his knife struck upon something.

Here we go!

What is it?

It's a box, I believe. Let's have a look at what's inside.

Man, it's money! There are gold coins worth thousands of dollars here!

Should we bury it again?

No, we'll take it to my den.

Number One?

No, Number Two. Under the cross.

Well, you don't need to do that other job now.

You don't understand. That one isn't about robbery, it's about revenge.

Lordy, Huck, you think he means us?

I hope not!

The next day, Tom snatched a hurried breakfast, and went to find Huck.

Rot him, Hucky. We should find him, track him, and track the money. That was going to be our treasure!

We'll never find him, Tom! Where's Number Two anyway?

Let me think, Hucky... it's not a house number in this town... maybe it's a room at a tavern!

That's it. There are only two taverns, so you'll find it quickly.

You stay here till I come back, Huck.

Tom did not want to have Huck's company in public places.

He was gone half an hour.

Huck, I think I found the Number Two we're after.

Now what are we going to do?

Let me think.

You get all the door keys you can, and I'll nip home. We'll go to Injun Joe's room tonight and try them. Keep a lookout and, if you see Injun Joe, follow him and figure out where he's going.

I'll follow him. I will, by jingoes!

Now you're talking! Don't you ever weaken, Huck, and nor will I.

That night, Tom and Huck began their adventure, but they had no luck. Tuesday and Wednesday brought similar luck, but Thursday night promised better.

AHHHHH!

Run... ...Huck, run! Run... ...for your... ...life!

What was it? What did you see?

Injun Joe! I walked in, and there he was!

He was lying there, sound asleep on the floor.

Hucky, let's not try that again till we know Injun Joe is not in there. If we watch every night, we'll see him go out. Then we'll snatch that box quicker than lightning.

I agree, Tom. I'll keep watch on that tavern every night for a year. I'll sleep all day and I'll stand watch all night.

PHIPPS TAVERN

The two adventurers agreed that, if Huck saw anything, he'd meow at Tom's window as usual.

The first thing Tom heard on Friday morning was a piece of good news— Judge Thatcher's family had come back to town the night before.

...and so, Mama said I could finally have my picnic.

And you'll come, won't you, Tom Sawyer?

Hmmm.

The ferry boat was hired to take the party upstream to the picnic's location.

Those present carried out every type of activity to get them all hot and tired. Then someone shouted...

Who's ready for the caves?

Bundles of candles were produced, and straightaway everyone scampered up the hill.

The party frolicked and explored within the cave.

Eventually, one group after another came struggling back to the mouth of the cave. They were panting, laughing, smeared from head to foot with clay, and entirely delighted with the success of the day.

TING TING TING

They had been taking no note of time and were astonished to find that night had fallen. The bell of the ferry boat had been clanging for half an hour.

TINGTINGTING

Nobody cared about the wasted time, except for the captain of the craft.

Elsewhere.

Is there any use? Is there really any use in waiting around here any longer?

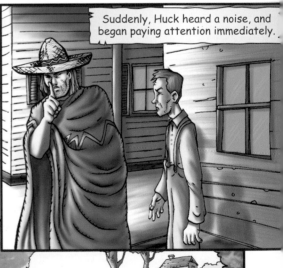

Suddenly, Huck heard a noise, and began paying attention immediately.

He stepped out and glided along behind the men, cat-like, with bare feet.

Huck knew where he was. He was approaching the gate leading into Widow Douglas's grounds.

The Widow Douglas. She's been kind to me. This must be that 'revenge' job they were on about.

Her husband was rough on me. He was the judge that jailed me. He also had me horsewhipped. Now she'll pay for it. I'll slit her nostrils and notch her ears like a sow.

Oh, don't kill her! Don't do that!

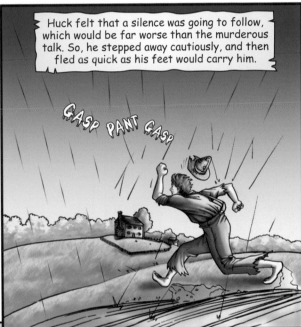

Huck felt that a silence was going to follow, which would be far worse than the murderous talk. So, he stepped away cautiously, and then fled as quick as his feet would carry him.

GASP PANT GASP

What's going on? Who's banging? What do you want?

Let me in. Quick! I'll tell you everything!

THUD THUD

Why, who are you?

Huckleberry Finn. Quick! Let me in!

By George, he must have something to tell, or he wouldn't act like this! Out with it, lad.

Three minutes later, the old man and his sons were on their way to Widow Douglas's. Huckleberry watched...

...and listened.

BLAM

It's alright, lad. They got away, but we got there in time. The Widow Douglas is fine.

Who were they, lad? You can trust me. I won't betray you.

It was Injun Joe!

Injun Joe! Well, that explains it. Don't you worry, boy, we'll get him.

You're burning up, lad.

I went back to the house to look for signs, but didn't find any. I only found a bulky bundle of--

Of what?

Of burglar's tools. What's the matter with you? What were you expecting us to find?

Umm. Sunday school books, maybe.

HEE HEE HAHA

Huck felt glad that they hadn't found the bundle he was thinking of. Everything seemed to be going in the right direction—the treasure must be in Number Two, Injun Joe would be captured and jailed that day, and he and Tom could seize the gold that night without any fear of interruption.

Poor old chap. You're pale and jaded. You aren't well at all, but you'll come out of it. Rest and sleep will make you better.

Meanwhile, talk had started before church. No one had noticed Tom and Becky on board the ferry boat on the way back from the picnic. After church, one young man finally blurted out his fear that they were still in the cave.

Tom Sawyer and Becky Thatcher!

Gone!

Not on the boat.

Oh, my Tom! He wasn't a bad boy!

Alarm swept through the village and, within five minutes, the bells were wildly clanging. Within half an hour, men were pouring down the road and river toward the cave.

Meanwhile...

Tom, Tom, we're lost! We're lost! We'll never get out of this awful place! Oh, why did we ever leave the others?

Let's go. We should keep trying.

After some time, the two lost souls stopped to eat the last of their cake, and drink from the nearby water.

We must stay here, Becky. There's water to drink, but this is our last candle.

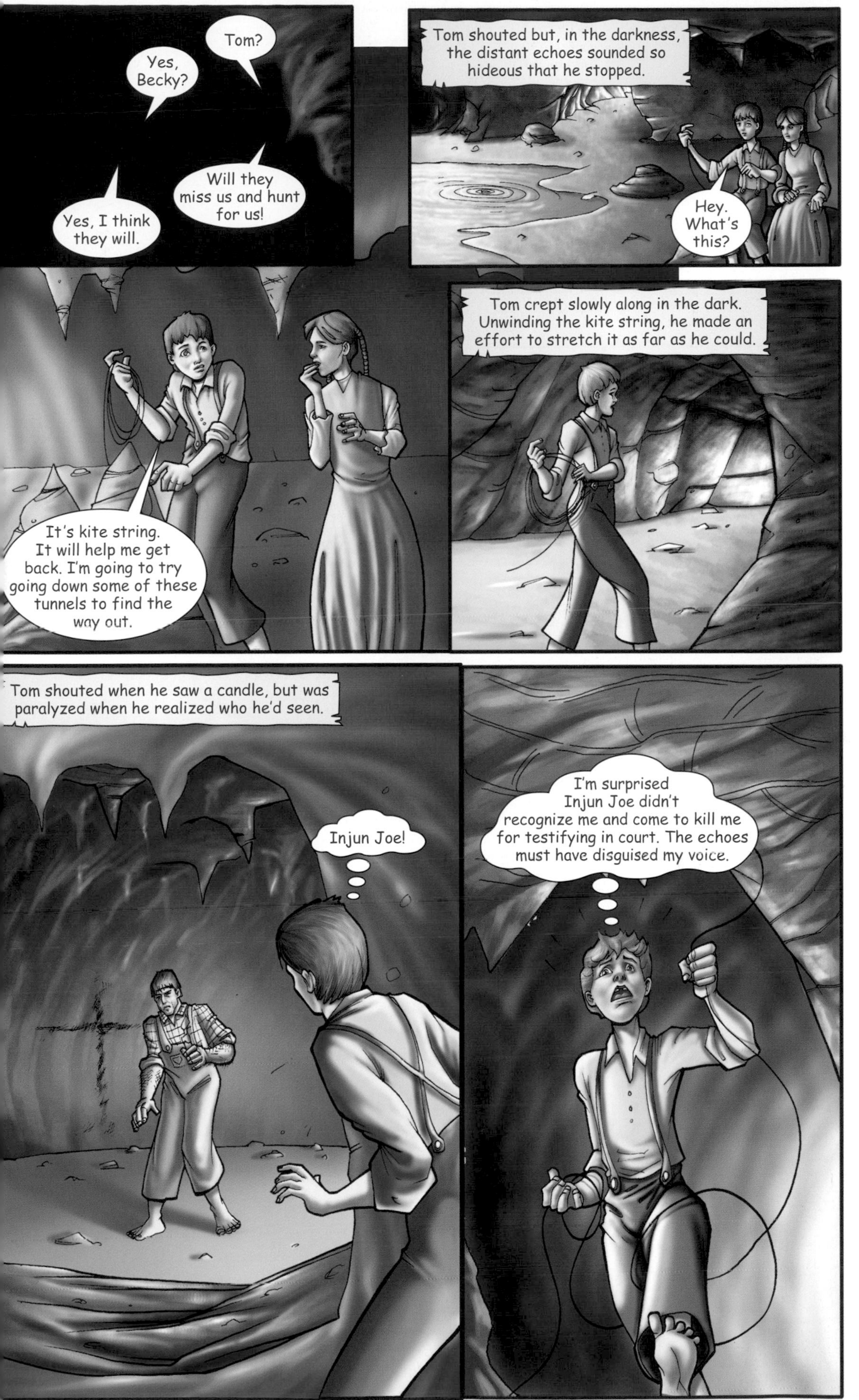
Tom?
Yes, Becky?
Will they miss us and hunt for us!
Yes, I think they will.
Tom shouted but, in the darkness, the distant echoes sounded so hideous that he stopped.
Hey. What's this?
It's kite string. It will help me get back. I'm going to try going down some of these tunnels to find the way out.
Tom crept slowly along in the dark. Unwinding the kite string, he made an effort to stretch it as far as he could.
Tom shouted when he saw a candle, but was paralyzed when he realized who he'd seen.
Injun Joe!
I'm surprised Injun Joe didn't recognize me and come to kill me for testifying in court. The echoes must have disguised my voice.

Did you find the way?

No. I'm trying again.

Tuesday afternoon came and went. The village of St. Petersburg still mourned. The lost children had not been found. Aunt Polly had become melancholy, and her gray hair had grown almost white.

HURRAY

Suddenly, a wild peal burst from the village bells and the streets were swarming with frantic people.

They've been found, they've been found!

Tom told the story of how they had escaped. While exploring the cave, he had seen a far-off spek that looked like daylight.

He had pushed his head and shoulders through a small hole, and had seen the Mississippi river rolling by. If it had been night, he would not have seen that spek of light.

Some men had come along in a skif and had taken them aboard. They had rowed to a house, given them supper, made them rest for two or three hours and then brought them home.

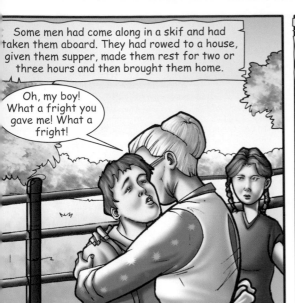

Oh, my boy! What a fright you gave me! What a fright!

Three days and nights of toil and hunger in the cave were not to be shaken off at once. Tom and Becky were bedridden all of Wednesday and Thursday, and seemed to grow more and more tired all the time.

About a fortnight after his rescue, Tom went to Judge Thatcher's house to see Becky.

Well, Tom, wouldn't you like to go to that cave again?

Yes! Yes, I would.

Well, there are others just like you, Tom. So, we have taken care of that. Nobody will get lost in that cave anymore.

Why?

Because I had its entrance covered with iron two weeks ago, and triple locked.

Tom turned as white as a sheet.

Oh no! Injun Joe was in there!

63

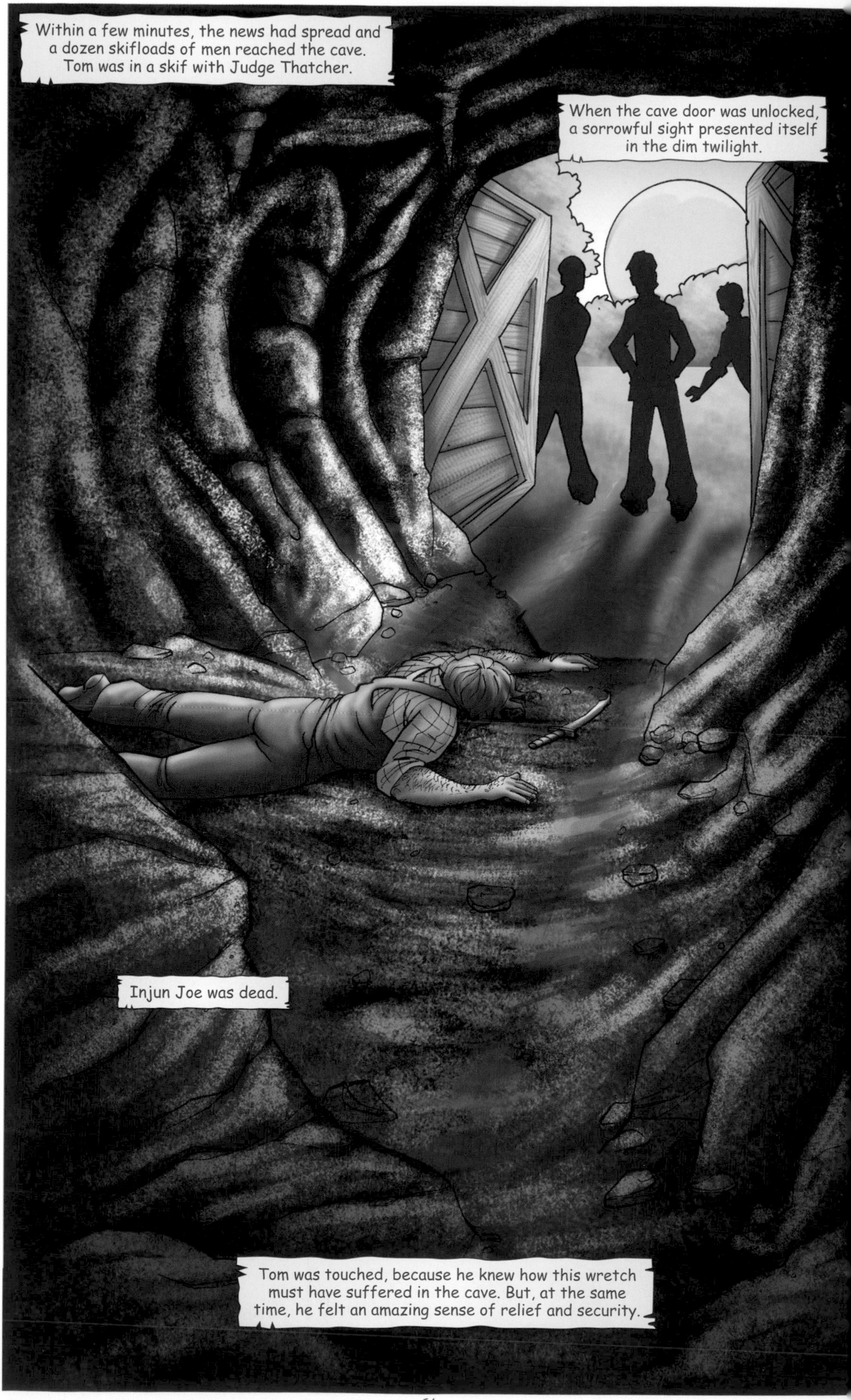
Within a few minutes, the news had spread and a dozen skifloads of men reached the cave. Tom was in a skif with Judge Thatcher.
When the cave door was unlocked, a sorrowful sight presented itself in the dim twilight.
Injun Joe was dead.
Tom was touched, because he knew how this wretch must have suffered in the cave. But, at the same time, he felt an amazing sense of relief and security.

Several days later...

I heard you were sick. Glad you're better.

Heard you were too. Glad you're up and about.

Hucky, there's one thing I didn't tell you. The money's in the cave, Huck! It's in the cave!

Tom, are you joking or being serious?

I'm serious, Huck. More serious than I've ever been in my life. Will you come there and help me to get it out?

You bet I will! I will if it's where we can find it and not get lost.

Huck, we can do that without the least bit of trouble.

Is it far inside the cave? I've been on my feet for three or four days, and I can't walk more than a mile. At least, I don't think I can.

It's about five miles inside the cave the way most people would go, Huck. But there's a short cut that nobody knows—except I!

It's just around here. All my life I've wanted to be a robber. And now I've got the chance.

There you go, Huck. It's the snuggest hole in this country. We'll be robbers—Tom Sawyer's Gang. It sounds splendid, doesn't it, Huck?

It does, Tom. And who will we rob?

Oh, almost anybody. Waylay people—that's usually the way.

Why, it's great, Tom. It sounds better than being a pirate.

Now, where's this Number Two? Under the cross, maybe? Hey, right there's where I saw Injun Joe with his candle, Huck!

Look here, Huck. There are footprints and some candle grease on one side of the rock, but not on the other sides. Why is that? I bet you the money is under the rock. I'm going to dig in the clay.

That isn't a bad idea, Tom!

THUNK

Got it, at last! We're rich, Tom!

My goodness, Huck, look here!

Before long, the boys were home with the bags of money. Aunt Polly was sitting with Widow Douglas and some other friends.

Come here, boys. We were just discussing Huckleberry.

Huck walked up to Widow Douglas. Her gratitude was visible, not only in her face, but also in her voice. She thanked him profusely.

I needed some way to say thank you for saving me from those robbers.

The widow has agreed to give Huck a home and have him educated. And when she can spare the money, she will start him in business.

Huck doesn't need all that. He's rich.

Huck's got money. Maybe you don't believe it, but he's got lots of it.

HAHAHA

The ladies could not hold back their laughter at the pleasant joke.

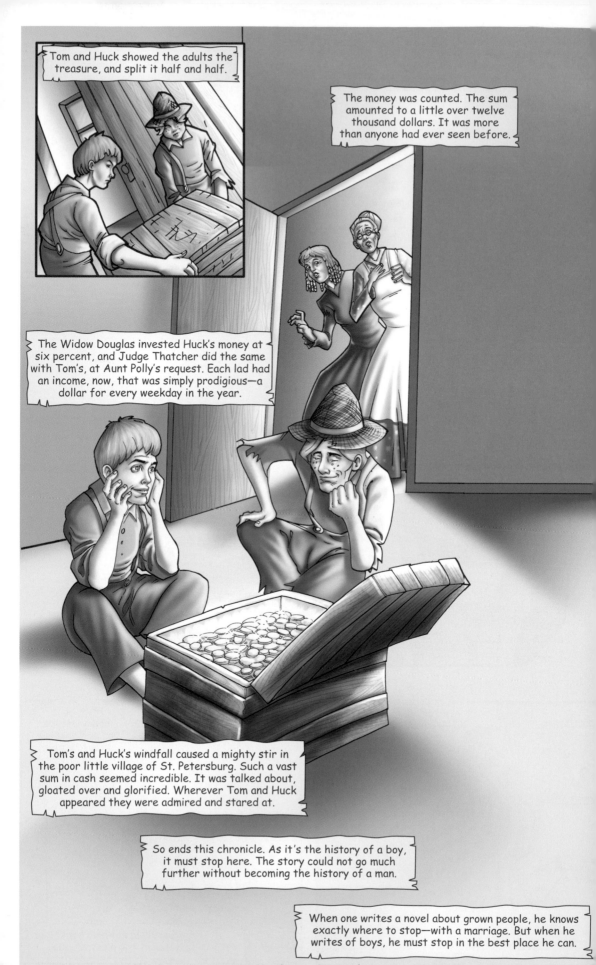

Tom and Huck showed the adults the treasure, and split it half and half.

The money was counted. The sum amounted to a little over twelve thousand dollars. It was more than anyone had ever seen before.

The Widow Douglas invested Huck's money at six percent, and Judge Thatcher did the same with Tom's, at Aunt Polly's request. Each lad had an income, now, that was simply prodigious—a dollar for every weekday in the year.

Tom's and Huck's windfall caused a mighty stir in the poor little village of St. Petersburg. Such a vast sum in cash seemed incredible. It was talked about, gloated over and glorified. Wherever Tom and Huck appeared they were admired and stared at.

So ends this chronicle. As it's the history of a boy, it must stop here. The story could not go much further without becoming the history of a man.

When one writes a novel about grown people, he knows exactly where to stop—with a marriage. But when he writes of boys, he must stop in the best place he can.

# ABOUT US

It is nighttime in the forest. The sky is black, studded with countless stars. A campfire is crackling, and the storytelling has begun—stories about love and wisdom, conflict and power, dreams and identity, courage and adventure, survival against all odds, and hope against all hope. In the warm, cheerful radiance of the campfire, the storyteller's audience is captivated, as in a trance. Even the trees and the earth and the animals of the forest seem to have fallen silent, bewitched.

Inspired by this enduring relationship between a campfire and gripping storytelling, we bring you four series of *Campfire Graphic Novels*:

Our *Classic* tales adapt timeless literature from some of the greatest writers ever.

Our *Mythology* series features epics, myths and legends from around the world, tales that transport readers to lands of mystery and magic.

Our *Biography* titles bring to life remarkable and inspiring figures from history.

Our *Original* line showcases brand new characters and stories from some of today's most talented graphic novelists and illustrators.

We hope you will gather around our campfire and discover the fascinating stories and characters inside our books.

CAMPFIRE™

#  ntriguing slands

## GUNKANJIMA: THE GHOST ISLAND OF JAPAN

Once an island bustling with activity and people, Gunkanjima now lies totally abandoned with crumbling streets and empty buildings. This island was famous for its coal mines during the 19th century. But when petroleum began replacing coal in the 1960s, the mines shut down and the people left the island. Today, even visitors to the island are forbidden. A very interesting fact is that Japan's first large concrete building was built on this island in 1916—a block of apartments to house the workers of the mine.

• The English translation of the name Gunkanjima is Battleship Island; so called because of the island's resemblance to a battleship.

## BISHOP ROCK

Bishop Rock is a small island in Britain. It has been listed as the smallest island in the world with a building, in the *Guinness World Records* book. It is only 46 meters long and 16 meters wide, and has a lighthouse on it which was built in 1858. Its light is automatically operated and nobody lives on the island. Since the island has no space for anything else besides the lighthouse, a helipad has been constructed on top of the structure for easier access.

• It is believed that, in the 13th century, convicts who committed grave crimes were dispatched to the rock, with only bread and water, and left to the mercy of the waves.

### DID YOU KNOW?
Islomania is an irresistible attraction to islands.
Authors such as Robert Louis Stevenson,
Jules Verne, Jack London and Joseph Conrad
were some famous islomaniacs!

## EASTER ISLAND

On Easter Sunday in 1722, a Dutch sailor, Jacob Roggeveen, and his crew landed on an unknown island in the Pacific close to Chile. They were stunned to find over 1,000 massive stone statues scattered all over the island, and about 2,000 people inhabiting it. Roggeveen called it Easter Island. It is believed that about 1,200 years ago, travelers came and settled on this island and carved the 'moai' out of volcanic rocks. The moai were gigantic statues of men, some as tall as a three-storeyed building. It is said that the entire population of the island was wiped out in the 1800s. What happened to them is still a mystery.

• Easter Island has an airstrip for the emergency landing of NASA space shuttles!

## ALCATRAZ, OR THE PRISON ISLAND

Alcatraz is located in San Francisco Bay, in the USA. It was named 'La Isla de los Alcatraces', which means 'Island of the Pelicans' by Spanish explorer, Juan de Ayala, in 1775. Popularly known as the 'Rock', it was most famous as a maximum security prison. The freezing waters and strong currents made it almost impossible for anyone to swim to the mainland. It closed down in 1934, and is now a very popular tourist spot.

- Al Capone, a famous Italian-American gangster, spent time in the prison in the 1930s. He used to play his banjo in the shower room during his days there. It is said that, since his death in 1947, people have heard the sound of a banjo coming from the empty shower rooms!

## THE WORLD ISLANDS AND THE PALM ISLANDS

If you fly over the waters of the Persian Gulf, close to Dubai in the UAE, and look down, you will see a very strange sight—a map of the world and two flattened palm trees on the water! If you go closer,

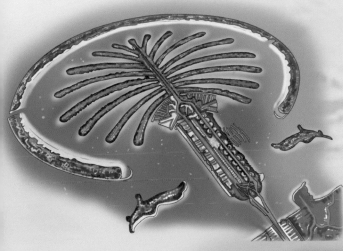

you'll see they are, in fact, man-made islands positioned to create these shapes. All these artificial islands are made of sand dragged from the bottom of the sea. The Palm Islands consist of three pieces of land in the shape of palm trees, while the World Islands consist of 300 islands laid out in the shape of a map of the world!

- There are plans to build 'The Universe', a set of artificial islands in the shape of the solar system, close to the World Islands.

**DID YOU KNOW?**
Australia is a continent, and a country, as well as an island! It is often called the island continent.